Dr. Seuss

HOORAY FOR DIFFENDOOFER DAY!

WITH SOME HELP FROM
Jack Prelutsky & Lane Smith

....

design by **Molly Leach**

ALFRED A. KNOPF · NEW YORK

I've always lived in Dinkerville,
My friends all live here too.
We go to Diffendoofer School—
We're happy that we do.

Our school is at the corner
Of Dinkzoober and Dinkzott.
It looks like any other school,
But we suspect it's not.
I think we're learning lots of things
Not taught at other schools.
Our teachers are remarkable,
They make up their own rules.

Miss Bobble teaches listening,
Miss Wobble teaches smelling.
Miss Fribble teaches laughing,
And Miss Quibble teaches yelling.

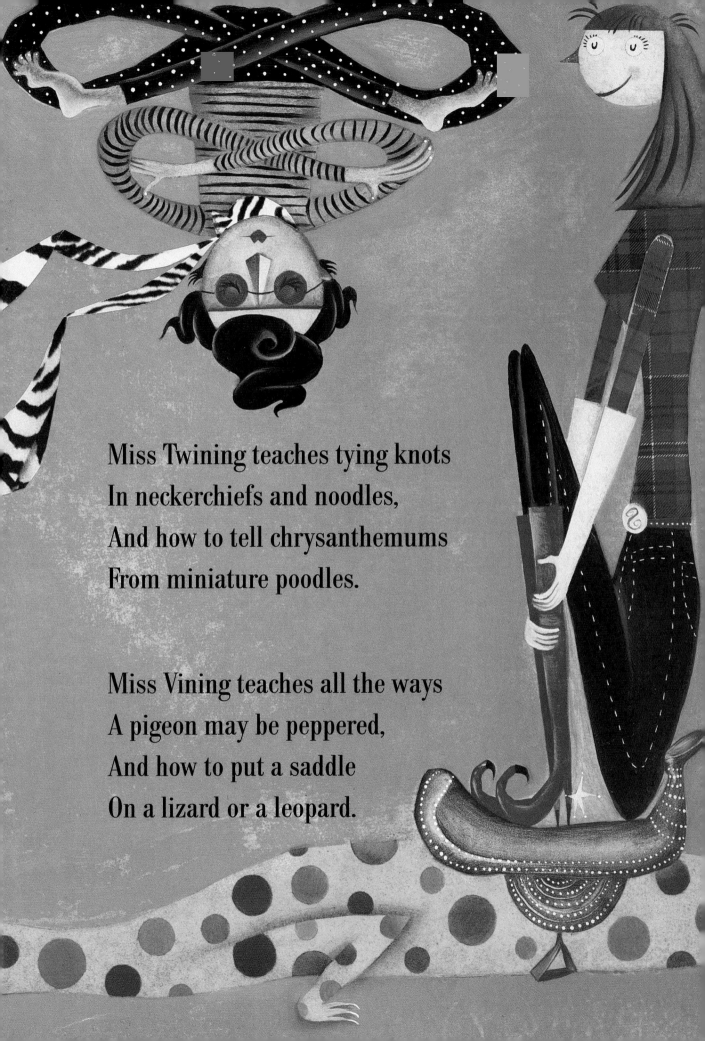

Miss Twining teaches tying knots
In neckerchiefs and noodles,
And how to tell chrysanthemums
From miniature poodles.

Miss Vining teaches all the ways
A pigeon may be peppered,
And how to put a saddle
On a lizard or a leopard.

My teacher is Miss Bonkers,
She's as bouncy as a flea.
I'm not certain what she teaches,
But I'm glad she teaches me.

"Look! Look!" she chirps. "I'll show you how
To tell a cactus from a cow,
And then I shall instruct you why
A hippo cannot hope to fly."

She even teaches frogs to dance,
And pigs to put on underpants.
One day she taught a duck to sing—
Miss Bonkers teaches EVERYTHING!

Of all the teachers in our school,
I like Miss Bonkers best.
Our teachers are all different,
But she's *different-er* than the rest.

We also have a principal,
His name is Mr. Lowe.
He is the very saddest man
That any of us know.
He mumbles, "Are they learning
This and that and such and such?"
His face is wrinkled as a prune
From worrying so much.

He breaks a lot of pencil points
From pushing down too hard,
And many dogs start barking
As he mopes around the yard.
We think he wears false eyebrows.
In fact, we're sure it's so.
We've heard he takes them
    off at night...
I guess we'll never know.

But we *know* he likes Miss Bonkers,
He treats her like a queen.
He's always there to watch her
When she's on her trampoline.

There are many other people
Who make Diffendoofer run.
They are utterly amazing—
I love every single one.

Our nurse, Miss Clotte,
        knows what to do
When we've got sniffles or the flu.
One day I had a splinter, so
She bandaged me from head to toe.

Mr. Plunger, our custodian,
Has fashioned a machine—
A super-zooper-flooper-do—
It keeps the whole school clean.

Nurse

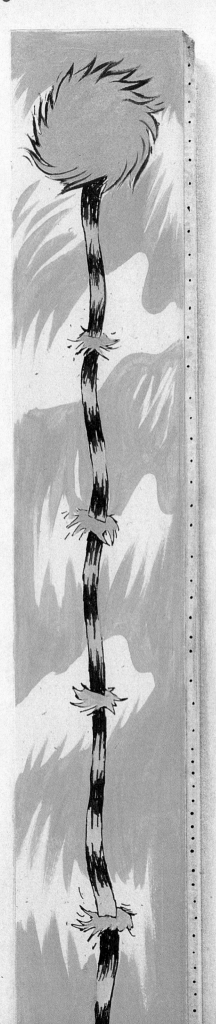

Our music teacher, Mrs. Fox,
Makes bagpipes out of
    straws and socks.
Our art instructor, Mr. Beeze,
Paints pictures hanging by his knees.

In science class with Mr. Katz,
We learn to build robotic rats.

In gym we watch as Mr. Bear
Hoists elephants into the air.

Miss Loon is our librarian,
She hides behind the shelves,
And often cries out, "LOUDER!"
When we're reading to ourselves.

We have three cooks, all named McMunch,
Who merrily prepare our lunch.
They make us hot dogs, beans, and fries,
Plus things we do not recognize.
And as they cook, they sing their song,
Not too short and not too long.
"Roast and toast and slice and dice,
Cooking lunch is oh so nice."

er
Cafeteria
Gym
Art
Z-2
E-i-O
?
Hither
A-1
Dither
Nurse
G
L-7
10-X
Music
YONDER
Principal
30-G
Library
Girls
L
Boys

We were eating their concoctions,
Telling jokes and making noise,
When Mr. Lowe appeared and howled,
"Attention, girls and boys!"

He began to fuss and fidget,
Scratch and mutter, sneeze and cough.
He shook his head so hard, we thought
His eyebrows *would* come off.
He wrung his hands, he cleared his throat,
He shed a single tear,
Then sobbed, "I've something to announce,
And that is why I'm here.

"All schools for miles and miles around
Must take a special test,
To see who's learning such and such—
To see which school's the best.
If our small school does not do well,
Then it will be torn down,
And you will have to go to school
In dreary Flobbertown."

"Not Flobbertown!" we shouted,
And we shuddered at the name,
For *everyone* in Flobbertown
Does *everything* the same.

It's miserable in Flobbertown,
They dress in just one style.
They sing one song, they never dance,
They march in single file.
They do not have a playground,
And they do not have a park.
Their lunches have no taste at all,
Their dogs are scared to bark.

Miss Bonkers rose. "Don't fret!" she said.
"You've learned the things you need
To pass that test and many more—
I'm certain you'll succeed.
We've taught you that the earth is round,
That red and white make pink,
And something else that matters more—
We've taught you how to think."

"I hope you're right," sighed Mr. Lowe.
He shed another tear.
"The test is in ten minutes,
And you're taking it right here."

We sat in shock and disbelief.
"Oh no!" we moaned. "Oh no!"
We were even more unhappy
Than unhappy Mr. Lowe.
But then the test was handed out.
"Yahoo!" we yelled. "Yahoo!"
For it was filled with all the things
That we all *knew* we knew.

There were questions about noodles,
About poodles, frogs, and yelling,
About listening and laughing,
And chrysanthemums and smelling.
There were questions about other things
We'd *never* seen or heard,
And yet we somehow answered them,
Enjoying every word.

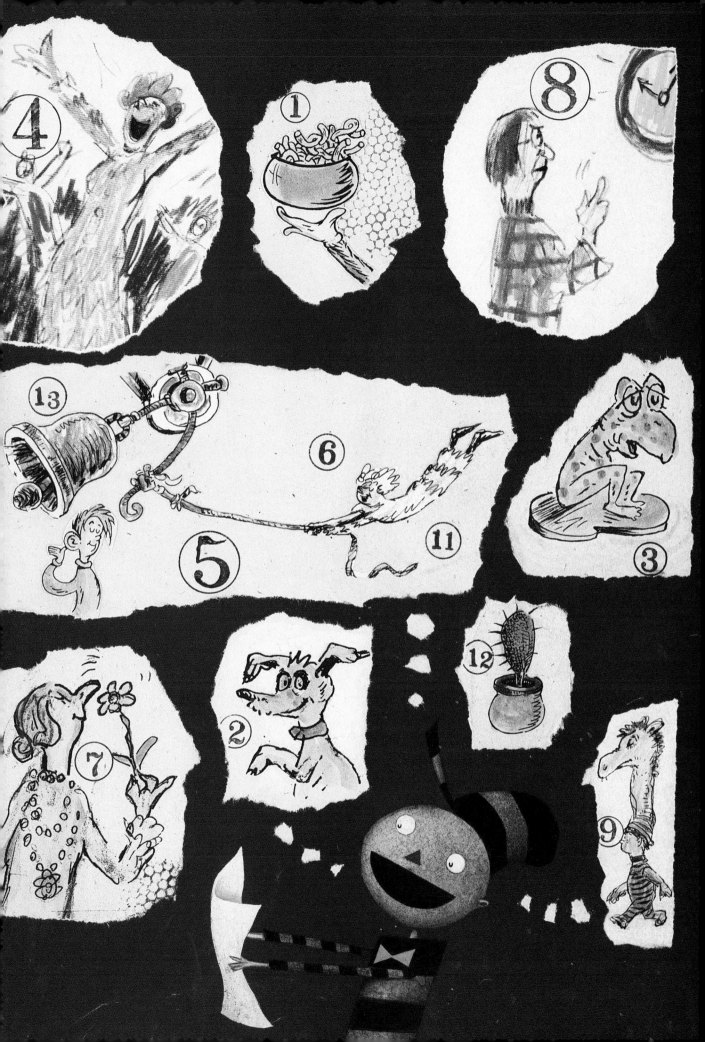

One week later, after recess,
Mr. Lowe meandered in.
We'd never seen him smile before,
But now he wore a grin.

He soon began to giggle,
Then his giggle grew by half,
And then it *really* happened—
Mr. Lowe began to laugh.

"You've saved our school!
You've saved our school!"
He jubilantly roared.
"We got the very highest score!"
He wrote it on the board.

Miss Bonkers did some cartwheels
Till her face turned cherry red.
She bounded up to Mr. Lowe
And kissed him on the head.
"Hooray! Hooray!" she shouted.
"I'm so proud I cannot speak."
So she did another cartwheel,
And she pecked him on the cheek.

"Ahem! Ahem!" coughed Mr. Lowe.
"You all deserve a bow.
I thus declare a holiday—
It starts exactly now.
Because you've done so splendidly
In every sort of way,
This day forever shall be known
As Diffendoofer Day.
And furthermore, I promise
I won't ever wear a frown.
For now I know we'll never go
To dreary Flobbertown."

Then we held a celebration,
There was pizza, milk, and cake.
Like everyone, I ate too much
And got a bellyache.
We laughed and whooped and hollered
The entire school day long,
Then we all sang, triumphantly,
"The Diffendoofer Song."

We love you, Diffendoofer School,
We definitely do.

There surely is no other school
That's anything like you.
You're *gribbulous*, you're *grobbulous*,
Each day we love you more.
You are the school we treasure
And unceasingly adore.

Oh, finest school in Dinkerville—
The only one as well—
We love you, Diffendoofer School,
Much more than we can tell.
You are so *diffendooferous*
It gives us joy to say,
Three cheers for Diffendoofer School—

How This Book Came To Be

Dr. Seuss—or Ted, as everyone called him, his real name being Theodor Seuss Geisel—usually didn't talk about what he was working on. Often we had no idea what the book was until he flew to New York to present us with a polished manuscript and the finished art. However, during a telephone chat in 1988 or 1989, when I asked him what he was doing, he did not sidestep the question with a humorous non-answer.

"Oh, I'm trying to do a book about a schoolteacher," he said. "But I'm not sure if teachers will like it." I assured him that teachers probably would like it. "Well, I don't know," he continued. "This teacher is pretty different." That was the first—and the last—I heard of the project, and within a year or so he submitted to me, his editor at Random House, *Oh, the Places You'll Go!*, his last work.

After Ted died in 1991, I asked his steadfast secretary, Claudia Prescott, to send me whatever he had done on the book about the teacher. "Oh, you mean Miss Bonkers!" she instantly responded, for that was how Ted had referred to it. "He had the sketches up on his bulletin board for a long time," Claudia said, "and he used to say, 'Miss Bonkers is driving me bonkers.'" Ted had taken a fancy to Miss Bonkers, and Claudia hoped that I would too.

When the package arrived, I ripped it open and read it in a rush. There were fourteen pages of wonderful colored-pencil sketches, each with a scrawled couplet or two in Ted's characteristic hand printing. Some pages had as many as four different sketches. The package also included a few other sheets of paper with lists of possible names for the school and places in the school, such as the lunchroom and the gym, where he planned to take the story.

Of all the teachers in our school
we like miss Bonkers best.
Our teachers all are different.
But She's different-er than the rest.

She is the one
who teaches how
to tell a cactus
from a cow.

We have to keep her
strong and well
so she can ring the Assembly Bell.

I wish you could go to my school
We're happy as can be.
Oh, ~~how happy you would be~~

(at tee William Wilkins Woofer Junior
El-e-menter-ee!)

(at the wonderful Woodrow Watkins Woofer
El-e-menter-ee!)
(at tee wonderful P.S. 22 thousand
nine hundred and sixty Rree.)

Zoofendorf Elementary
Zinzendorf School

~~Zzz~~   Eezeekiel

Woodrow Waldo Woodruff Jr.
J. Ebeneezer Bomberg Jr.
Ebeneezer Woofer Jr.
Woodrow Watkins Woofer, Jr.
Woodrow ~~Watkins~~ Wilkens Watson Jr
William Wadsworth (Wheeler,) Jr.
  Waldo Wordsworth (Woofer)
Waldo Wilkins Woofer, Jr
Waldo Watkins Woofer, Jr.

    Henry Hawkins Hoofer, Jr
  Waldo Woodruff Watkins Jr.

Waldo
Watkins
Woofer
Jr.

P.S. 22,963

* P.S.
  15,263

Zinzin
Zinzinsdorff

at tee
tw
Woofenberg
Elementary

Z

merrily
Jubilee

be
see
all of it is free
suits me to a T.
gee
whee!
A.B.C.
D.
Flea
Knee
three
me
tree

Our Principal
is mr. Ladd.
He sort of makes us
sort of sad.

~~we think his feet~~
We think his big toe
hurts quite bad.

We're sorry for
poor mr. Ladd.

Principal

Though I loved what I saw, my heart sank. I had harbored the hope that Ted had actually completed a story, but he had not gotten that far. He had created some characters, a setting, and a few verses. Though it didn't add up to a book, there was definitely something there and something so fresh, funny, and, in a way I couldn't possibly explain, *important* about these sketches that I wanted to find a way to publish it. But I was baffled as to how to do it. Doctoring Dr. Seuss was something I had never had to do during the eleven years I was his editor.

So I did as Ted had done—put it aside and went on to something else. Every once in a while I would pull out the file and look at the sketches again. Finally it dawned on me that what he had been trying to do was write a story in celebration of individuality and creative thinking. Light bulbs began flashing: Why not ask children's poet Jack Prelutsky and children's book illustrator Lane Smith to finish what Ted had started? If anyone could do it,

But we know
he likes miss Bonkers.
He thinks she's pretty keen.

He comes outside
to watch her
when she's on the trambolene

Our Janitor is Mr. Snow.
~~For some strange reason we don't know~~
He dresses like an Eskimo.
~~Why he does it we don't know~~

He loves to sit outside his door
and fish ~~right inside~~ here in the corridor.
He catches them right through the floor.

this tremendously talented and free-spirited pair could. They both resemble third-grade classroom cut-ups, the kind of wise guys in the back of the room whom Ted admired but was always too shy to join, at least not in public. They are funny and they are original. I knew I could count on them not to simply imitate Dr. Seuss, though they are big fans of his—so, yes, why not ask them?

Finding a plot was the first critical step, and once Jack hit upon a kind of modern-day achievement test that the students at Diffendoofer School had to pass—or be sent to dreary Flobbertown—I knew the nut had been cracked. In addition to creating from scratch the majority of the verses (though a number of Ted's verses were used verbatim), there were many decisions of varying magnitude for Jack to make: for example, which custodian of the two conceptualized by Dr. Seuss should stay in the book; indeed, what school name from the more than twenty jotted down by Dr. Seuss should be the chosen one (Jack picked "Diffendoof" because it suggests the word "different"; he added the "er" ending because the extra beat fit better into his own rhyme scheme).

> If you take your turn
> oh the things you can learn
> at Zinzendoof Elementary.
> Diffendoof Elementary
> Ziffendoof

Lane used the body of Dr. Seuss's illustration—his striped and whirling fantasylands, his zigs and zags and bursts of color—plus his original sketches as inspiration. Combining collage with oil painting, Lane had fun working into the story a few cameo appearances by famous Dr. Seuss characters, images, and books.

We know he likes miss Bonkers.
cause he tries to give her fish.

But we don't think mr. Snow will get her.
We think she likes mr. Lodd much better

She calls our Janitor, mr. Green
who spics things up real neat and clean —
with his handy vacu-bike machine.

With *Hooray for Diffendoofer Day!* Jack and Lane do indeed pay homage to Dr. Seuss, but in their own distinctive way. The result is the union of three one-of-a-kind voices in a book that is greater than the sum of its parts.

I have a hunch that Ted's unfinished story about the unsinkable Miss Bonkers and the very different school she was a part of led him to *Oh, the Places You'll Go!* When he got stuck trying to praise those who teach us how to think, he simply leapfrogged to how we'll be called upon to use those "brains in our head and feet in our shoes" after graduation day.

Miss Finkel teaches Arithmetic.

Miss Winkel teaches **Smelling.**

MissYonkers teaches the clock toftc

missBonkers teaches Yelling.

Out in the School of Life (which is the setting for *Oh, the Places You'll Go!*),
I think Miss Bonkers's class and all the graduates of Diffendoofer School
would indeed succeed—98 and 3/4 percent guaranteed!

So thank you, Jack and Lane, for making it possible for Miss Bonkers to have her day in class.

Janet Schulman
New York, April 1998

In memory of Dr. Seuss
–Jack Prelutsky & Lane Smith

This is a Borzoi Book published by Alfred A. Knopf

Text in body of work copyright © Dr. Seuss Enterprises, L.P., and Jack Prelutsky 1998.

Text in afterword copyright © 1998 by Alfred A. Knopf.

Illustrations in body of work copyright © Lane Smith 1998. Representations in Lane Smith's illustrations of original and modified Dr. Seuss characters ™ & copyright © Dr. Seuss Enterprises, L.P. Used by permission.

Illustrations in afterword copyright © Dr. Seuss Enterprises, L.P. 1998.

www.randomhouse.com

Book design by Molly Leach

Printed in the United States

Library of Congress Cataloging-in-Publication Data
Seuss, Dr.
Hooray for Diffendoofer Day! / by Dr. Seuss and Jack Prelutsky ; illustrated by Lane Smith.
p.   cm.
Summary: The students of Diffendoofer School celebrate their unusual teachers and curriculum,
including Miss Fribble, who teaches laughing, Miss Bonkers, who teaches frogs to dance,
and Mr. Katz, who builds robotic rats.
ISBN 0-679-89008-4 (trade). — ISBN 0-679-99008-9 (lib. bdg.)
[1. Teachers—Fiction. 2. Schools—Fiction. 3. Stories in rhyme.]
I. Prelutsky, Jack. II. Smith, Lane, ill. III. Title.
PZ8.3.G276Hm 1998
[E]—dc21
97-39725